'Goldi and her Locks' is the first in the Ju

For Boudicea,

Let's make things *just* right.

Written by Claudia Vowles

Illustrated by Claudia Vowles and Jonathan Pasquali

Art and Design by Bhagya Rathnaweera

Edited by Teodora Reavley and Nicky Willsher

A CIP catalogue record for this title is available from the British Library

ISBN 9798421209621

@justrightbookseries

Goldilocks pushed open the front door of the crooked wooden house and stepped inside.

There, on the kitchen table, were three bowls of steaming porridge.

Goldilocks reached for the biggest bowl and shovelled in a large spoonful.
"Ouch," Goldilocks spat, "that is too hot!"
She grabbed the medium bowl.

"Ergh," Goldilocks groaned, "that is too cold."
She reached for the smallest bowl and took a bite.
"Mmmm, that is *just right*."

In the sitting room, Goldilocks tested the wooden chairs. One was too hard. The other one was too soft. But the third and final chair was *just right*. Goldilocks stretched back in the little wooden chair.

With an almighty creak, the back snapped, and she rolled right off and onto the floor. "Stupid old chair," she said kicking the broken pieces.

Feeling weary from the porridge scoffing and chair breaking, she headed upstairs.
"I deserve a little lie-down," she said, launching herself at the first bed.
She landed with a thud.
"Ouch," she squealed, "this bed is too hard!"
The second was not to her liking either, and she groaned as she sunk deep into the centre of the bed.
But the third bed felt *just right.* So Goldilocks fell fast asleep.

Not before long, the Three Bears returned home.
"Someone has eaten all of my porridge!" exclaimed Baby Bear, "and someone has broken my chair, mummy!" he cried.
"Stay behind me," whispered Daddy Bear as the bear family climbed the staircase.

Daddy Bear hesitated before slowly pushing the bedroom door open. All three bears looked on in disbelief at the sight of Goldilocks asleep in Baby Bear's bed.

"Excuse me!" Daddy Bear said, clearing his throat.

Goldilocks awoke and, in an instant, jumped defensively from the bed.

"Ahhhhh!" she screamed, "get away from me you horrible bears, you're scaring me!"
Goldilocks barged past the bears and ran down the stairs.

"I'm calling the townsmen!" she shouted over her shoulder, slamming the door behind her.

Daddy Bear shook his head, picked up the pieces of Baby Bear's chair, and headed out to his workshop to fix it.

Goldilocks ran all the way home.
She stopped to catch her breath, when she noticed Three Little Pigs building a house made of straw.
"Silly pigs," Goldilocks rolled her eyes in disgust.

"Hello townsmen, I would like to report threatening behaviour."
"Can you give us a description, madam?" the townsman asked.
"Oh, yes. They were big, and hairy, and grizzly, and there were three of them!"

"We know the kind you're talking about," the townsman replied, "don't fear madam, we have it in hand."
Goldilocks replaced the receiver and nodded her head in delight.

The Three Little Pigs were putting the final touches on their house made of straw when a big bad wolf appeared.
"This should be interesting," Goldilocks said to herself.

"Little pig, little pig, let me come in."
"Not by the hairs on my chinny chin chin."
"Then I'll huff, and I'll puff, and I'll blow your house in."
So the wolf huffed, and he puffed, and he blew the house in.
The Three Little Pigs ran away with their little pink tails
between their little pink legs.
Goldilocks laughed to herself, "Good riddance, smelly pigs."

The next day the Little Pigs reappeared, and this time, they built their house out of sticks.

"Little pig, little pig, let me come in," called the wolf.

"Not by the hairs on my chinny chin chin."

"Then I'll huff, and I'll puff, and I'll blow your house in."

So the wolf huffed, and he puffed, and he blew the house in.

Once again, the Three Little Pigs ran away with their little pink tails between their little pink legs.

Goldilocks looked on through her kitchen window and let out a chuckle.

This time the Little Pigs came back with a truck-full of bricks.
They built the strongest, biggest, grandest house on the street.
The wolf huffed, and he puffed, and didn't blow their house in.
After hours of huffing and puffing, he finally gave up and disappeared into the deep, dark woods.

Goldilocks crossed her arms and stamped her feet.
"How dare those Little Pigs build the grandest house on my street," she scowled. "I am going to complain to the townsmen and have these pigs evicted."

Goldilocks reached for the phone.

"Thankfully, the townsmen have driven those pigs out of town," Goldilocks called over to the neighbours, "so I have decided to buy their house."

Goldilocks was out on pasture behind her new house, feeding her cow Maisy

She noticed a flock of sheep walking in circles on the nearby hillside.

"Can I help you?" Goldilocks called to the sheep.

"Baa!" answered the sheep.

"Dumb sheep," Goldilocks scowled making her way towards them across the field.

"Are you lost?" Goldilocks asked.
"We are looking for Little Bo Peep," replied one of the sheep.
"She has lost us and doesn't know where to find us," called another.
"Oh, Little Bo Peep!" Goldilocks exclaimed, "I went to school with Bo. She always struck me as the type to lose her sheep."

Goldilocks' mind wandered back to when she was a little girl.
"Bo Peep thinks she's so cool," Goldi said to her friends. "She's always playing football, and making everybody laugh," Goldi huffed. "Well let's see if I can make everyone laugh."

Hey Bo."

Hey Goldi," Bo Peep greeted her warily.

You wanna come and do some skipping with us?" Goldilocks asked.

Yeah, sure. I'll just finish my game and come over," replied Bo.

We will wait for you," smirked Goldi.

Thanks, Goldi," Bo smiled.

Well, we can hardly start without you. We need to use one of your locks as the skipping rope."

Goldi's friends burst into fits of laughter.

The next day, Bo Peep was sat quietly at the side of the playground. She didn't feel like playing football today.

"Oh, wow Goldi, your hair looks amazing," one of Goldi's friends cooed. "Yeah, so cool," chimed another.

"Thanks guys. I needed a change," said Goldi tossing her new hairstyle from side to side, "you can call me Goldilocks from now on." Goldilocks smiled over at Little Bo Peep. Little Bo Peep wiped a hot tear from her cheek.

Goldilocks snapped out of her daydream.
"Well as it happens, I am looking for some new sheep myself."
Goldilocks began to herd the sheep back towards the brick house when, suddenly, she was startled by a voice coming from the hillside.
"Hey Goldi, where are you going with my sheep?"

"Bo Peep? Long time no see."

"Where are you taking my sheep?" called Little Bo Peep.

"They told me you had lost them and didn't know where to find them," replied Goldilocks.

"So you thought that you would take them? Just like you stole? my hairstyle?" Bo Peep was annoyed.

"Calm down Bo."

Goldilocks flicked her locks over her shoulder. "It looks better on me anyway," she argued,turning to leave.
Little Bo Peep shook her head and led her sheep back over the hill.

When Goldilocks arrived back at her big brick house, there was a notice on the door: Goldilocks angrily banged on the door.

The Three Little Pigs answered.
"Can we help you?" Daddy Pig asked.

"What are you doing in my house?" squealed Goldilocks.

"I think you will find that this is our house," replied Daddy Pig, closing the door.

Goldilocks slumped down onto the floor and began to cry.
"What have I done to deserve this?" she sobbed. "This is just not right!"
Then, it suddenly dawned on her.

Goldilocks stood once more in front of a crooked wooden house in the clearing of a forest.
She knocked timidly on the door but there was no answer.
Goldilocks wandered over to the workshop.
"Hello?" called Goldilocks.
A big bear appeared in the doorway.
"Can I help you?" Mummy Bear asked peering down at Goldilocks.

"Your furniture is beautiful," Goldilocks said looking around.

"Thank you. We make it ourselves," said Mummy Bear, "This is where we fixed the chair you broke."

"About that. I have come to say I'm sorry," Goldilocks said, almost whispering.

"You nearly put us out of business when you reported us to the townspeople, after you broke into our house," said Mummy Bear.

"I am truly sorry. Could I buy some pieces of furniture from you?" Goldilocks pleaded.

Goldilocks bought the bears' handmade furniture, and shared them with all her followers. Soon, the three bears' business was booming, and Goldilocks returned home feeling quite pleased with herself.

The next morning a letter arrived.

Dear Goldilocks,
You broke into our house and accused us of being aggressive. You turned the townspeople against us and almost destroyed our business. You made our son feel unsafe in his own home. We cannot forgive you for that.
Privilege should not be wielded like a sword, but carried like a torch to illuminate others.
Yours kindly,
The Three Bears.

Goldilocks felt her face flush with embarrassment. She was sad that the Three Bears didn't forgive her, but she understood their reasons. She promised herself that from that day on, she would do whatever she could to make changes for the better.

Goldilocks looked over to the brick house that she once tried to claim for herself. She was happy to see The Three Little Pigs enjoying the home that they had worked so hard to build and protect. Goldilocks waved at Bo Peep and, for the first time, Bo waved back.

Goldilocks did not live happily ever after.
She knew that sometimes she had been unkind and had even benefitted from that unkindness.
But she felt hopeful that one day things would be *just right.*

Printed in Great Britain
by Amazon

78193537R00020